HALLOWEEN SKY RIDE

by ELIZABETH SPURR

illustrated by ETHAN LONG

Holiday House / New York

Text copyright © 2005 by Elizabeth Spurr
Illustrations copyright © 2005 by Ethan Long
All Rights Reserved
Printed in the United States of America
www.holidayhouse.com
First Edition
1 3 5 7 9 10 8 6 4 2

Library of Congress Cataloging-in-Publication Data
Spurr, Elizabeth.
Halloween sky ride / by Elizabeth Spurr ; illustrated by Ethan Long.— 1st ed.
p. cm.
Summary: Mildred the witch picks up one too many guests
on her broom on the way to a Halloween feast.
ISBN 0-8234-1870-7 (hardcover)
[1. Halloween—Fiction. 2. Witches—Fiction. 3. Stories in rhyme.]
I. Long, Ethan, ill. II. Title.
PZ8.3.S772Hal 2005
[E]—dc22
2003068584

ISBN-13: 978-0-8234-1870-1
ISBN-10: 0-8234-1870-7

For Stephie,
my No. 4 ghostie
E. S.

Hey, Larry! Isn't this fun?
WHEEEE!!!
E. L.

Witch Mildred was invited
to the wondrous Witches' Wobble,
a Halloween festivity
where witches go to gobble.

Her snakeskin invitation
read:

Feasting starts at Eight!

A Grand Buffet
(with Skunk Filet!)

She must not be late!

Hopping on her broomstick,
she took off from a thicket.
She raced along the back roads
to dodge a speeding ticket.

A skeleton soon hailed her.
(His bones could use some meat!)
He pled, "Please! I'm so hungry,
I rattle head to feet."

A jack-o'-lantern hollered,
"Please take me from this wall,
for some, I dread, might use my head
as a soccer ball."

Soon the three encountered
a ghost who was in tears.
"Please take me from this graveyard.
It's much too spooky here."

A shaky, quaky mummy
called, "I'm ready to collapse.
Please find me a warm hearthside,
for I forgot my wraps!"

A bat swooped down upon them.
He squeaked, "Please wait for me!
I'll go batty when the sexton bongs
the bells in my belfry."

A black cat yowled,
"Please take me.
I need some company,
for when I cross their pathways,
people run from me!"
The six squeezed close together
to make room for the cat.
But the broomstick broke midair.
The riders tumbled–

"I'm sorry," said the kitty.
"I've wrecked your broomstick ride."
"No matter," said Witch Mildred.
"We're here. Let's go inside!"

WITCHES' WOBBLE

The clock atop the castle
read twenty after eight,
but the promised buffet table
held only emptied plates!
"No eye of newt? No sautéed slug?
No pickleworm pâté?

No casserole of cockroach!
No spiderweb soufflé!
Those greedy gobbling goblins
left zilch for us to eat."
Said the starving skeleton,
"Why don't we trick-or-treat?"

They passed a lighted cottage,
from which rose song and lauger.
The mummy boldly rang the be
all others traipsing after.

The children squealed and giggled
as they greeted their new guests,
for of all the trick-or-treaters,
these costumes were the best!

The hostess asked the callers
to join them at their party.
"Check out this spread!" the mummy said.
The hostess said, "Eat hearty."

"Taffy apples! Candy corn!
Purple punch, ice-cold!
My tongue's not touched such tastiness
since I was six years old!"

In the corner of the kitchen
Witch Mildred found a mop.
"I think this will do nicely
while my broom is in the shop."

"May I, please?" asked Mildred,
and seated her new friends.
With a loud "Thank you!" away they flew,
in loopy swoops and bends.

That night Witch Mildred dreamed
of cakes and lemonade,
but far more sweet than party treats
were the friendships she had made!